Modern Curriculum Press
BEGINNING TO READ Series

MODERN CURRICULUM PRESS

Ronald's Report Card

Alvin Granowsky
Craig L. Tweedt
Joy Ann Tweedt

Illustrated by Michael L. Denman

MODERN CURRICULUM PRESS
Cleveland • Toronto

© **1986 MODERN CURRICULUM PRESS, INC.**
13900 Prospect Road, Cleveland, Ohio 44136.

Softcover edition published simultaneously in Canada by Globe/ Modern Curriculum Press, Toronto.

Library of Congress Cataloging in Publication Data

Granowsky, Alvin, 1936-
  Ronald's report card.

  Summary: Since he is doing much better in school, Ronald is disappointed when a mistake on the computer causes his report card to show low grades.
  1. Children's stories, American. (1. Grading and marking (Students) — Fiction. 2. Schools — Fiction. 3. Computers — Fiction)   I. Tweedt, Craig L., 1950-   .   II. Tweedt, Joy Ann, 1951-   .   III. Denman, Michael L., ill.   IV. Title.
PZ7.G76664Rr   1985   (E)   85-8800

ISBN 0-8136-5164-6
ISBN 0-8136-5664-8 (pbk.)

    4 5 6 7 8 9 10   90 89

"Dad! Dad! Did my report card come in the mail?" Ronald ran into the house. "I just saw the letter carrier. Did he bring my report card?"

"Let's see," Dad said. "Oh, yes, your report card is here. Well, let's take a look." Dad opened the letter as he spoke.

"I can't wait to see my grades!" Ronald said. "I think I'm doing better in everything. Last week Mrs. James said that I'm becoming a good reader. She said that I'm getting better in math and spelling, too. Dad, I can't wait to see my report card!"

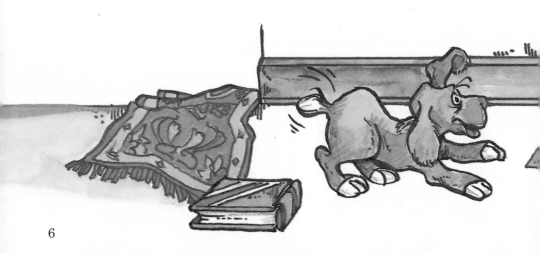

Ronald's father looked at the report card.
He didn't say anything, but the smile left
his face.

"Don't I have a good report card, Dad?
Mrs. James said I was doing much better."
Ronald saw the unhappy look on his
father's face.

His father slowly shook his head. "Ronald, why didn't you tell your mother and me that you were having problems in school?"

"But I'm not having problems, Dad."

Ronald's father handed him the report card. "Your grades have gone down in reading and math and spelling."

Ronald's eyes grew wide. "This can't be right. I thought I was doing so much better. Mrs. James used to have other children help me. Now she asks me to help others. I don't understand."

Ronald's father shook his head. "Your mother and I will have to see Mrs. James. We'll try to see her after school tomorrow when your mother comes home from work. She'll be able to tell us how we can help you."

Tears rolled from Ronald's eyes.
"Mrs. James said I was doing so much better.
She said she was proud of the way I was
working. Why didn't she tell me that I
was still having problems?"

The next morning in school, Ronald looked very sad. He couldn't laugh or even smile. He couldn't tell jokes with his friends. He didn't even want to talk to anyone because he felt so upset.

15

In the reading group, Ronald listened as the other children read. When Mrs. James called on him to read, he didn't make even one mistake.

"That's very good, Ronald!" Mrs. James said.

Ronald looked over all his words before
he handed in his spelling paper. He was
sure he had spelled all the words right.
Maybe he was having problems and didn't
know it.

"Mrs. James, did I spell my words
right?"

His teacher looked at his paper and
smiled. "You don't have one mistake!" she
said.

Ronald finished his math before the others. He took his paper up to his teacher. "Mrs. James, would you please look at my paper now?"

Mrs. James looked over the math paper. "Ronald, you have one mistake over here. Take a look at this and see if you can correct it yourself. If you take 6 away from 14, what do you have left?"

Ronald thought and thought. Then he remembered. "Eight! The answer is eight!"

"That's right," smiled Mrs. James. "Now take your paper and correct the mistake."

Ronald sat at his desk thinking about the mistake on his math paper. "Was it so bad to make a mistake?" Ronald thought. "Everyone makes mistakes sometimes."

When it was time to go outside to play, Ronald just sat at his desk.

"Come on, Ronald," his friends called. "Let's go outside to play!"

"I don't want to go outside," Ronald said. "I don't feel much like playing." He still felt upset about his report card.

Mrs. James came over to Ronald. "Don't you want to go outside with the other children?"

Ronald shook his head.

"Are you feeling sick?" his teacher asked. "You seem so unhappy."

"I'm unhappy about my report card,
Mrs. James. I thought I was doing so much
better in reading and math and spelling."

Mrs. James looked very surprised.
"What are you saying, Ronald? You **are**
doing better! You had a wonderful
report card!"

"Here, let me show you." Mrs. James went to her grade book. "Look at all the good grades you have!"

"But Mrs. James, my grades were not good on my report card. Didn't you write that report card?"

Mrs. James looked very upset. "Well, I sent your grades to the office. Then someone typed the grades into the computer. The computer printed your grades on the report card. Someone must have made a mistake. I will have to take care of this right away!"

25

Mrs. James met Ronald's mother and father after school.

"Hello," his teacher said, "I am so happy to see you again. I want you to know that I love having Ronald in my class. He is such a nice boy and he works very hard!"

Ronald's mother looked sad. She handed the report card to Mrs. James.

"We didn't know Ronald was having problems. He told us he was doing well."

"And he is doing well!" Mrs. James took the report card from Ronald's mother. "This report card is a mistake! Someone typed the wrong grades into the computer."

Then Mrs. James handed a new report card to Ronald's mother. "This is Ronald's report card!"

Ronald's mother and father looked at the new report card. Big smiles came over their faces. "Why, this report card is wonderful!"

Mrs. James said, "I am so sorry this mistake happened."

"We are so happy that it was just a mistake on the computer!" said Ronald's father.

"And we are pleased that Ronald is doing well in school!" Ronald's mother was smiling.

"I didn't know computers made mistakes," said Ronald.

"They don't," said Mrs. James, "but people who use them do. Someone typed in the wrong grades.

"But we **can** correct mistakes. And that's exactly what we've done."